Santa's Toy Shop

Classic Holiday Collection

written by Dandi
illustrated by Tammie Speer-Lyon

Santa's toy shop buzzed with activity. Only two days until Christmas Eve, when Santa would load the presents in his sleigh and deliver them to children around the world!

Elves hammered nails in rocking horses and doll houses. Even Mrs. Santa Claus helped. She sat by a snow-framed window and put the last stitches in a brand new baseball.

Ellie, the youngest of Santa's helpers, sat in a pile of wrapping paper. She wanted to do her bes wrapping gifts.

Then, maybe Santa would let her be a toy maker next Christmas. How she would love to make dolls and bikes and toy cars!

"Santa," Ellie said as she tucked in another gift. "I'm worried."

"Only two days left and still no letter from Danny. How will I know what gift to wrap for him?"

"You must do your best, Ellie," Santa said.

"Mail call!" Mrs. Claus shouted from the window.
"Here comes Elf Edward on Blitzen."

Edward handed the letters to Santa.

"Ellie!" Santa called. "There's a letter from Danny.
He wants a skateboard."

"That was close!" said Ellie. She picked a bright green skateboard from the elf assembly line. Next she wrapped the skateboard and stuffed it into Santa's pouch.

Now it was the day before Christmas Eve. Elves put a last minute shine on trumpets and trains. Shiny shoes got new laces. Other elves tried out the latest computer games. Ellie wrapped and wrapped.

Just then the door to the toy shop burst open, nearly knocking Santa down. "Well, upon my whiskers, Edward!" said Santa.

"Sorry, Santa," cried Edward. "I knew you'd want to see this right away!" He handed Santa another letter from Danny.

Ellie tried to look over Santa's shoulder as he read:

Dear Santa,
I told Mom about the skateboard. She said,
"NO WAY!" Would you please bring me
a ten-speed bike instead?"
    Love,
        DANNY

Ellie rushed to Santa's pouch and dumped it on the
toy shop floor. She pulled out the skateboard, wrapped a
blue racing bike, and stuffed it into the bag.
It wasn't easy!

Christmas Eve day the elves groomed the reindeer. Mrs. Claus packed Santa a midnight snack. And Ellie sat alone in the workshop tieing bows on the last packages.

This time it was Santa who burst in with another letter from Danny:

Dear Santa,
I'm really not big enough for a ten-speed. I thought about asking for one of your reindeer, but you need them. So if it's not too much trouble, please just surprise me.
Your friend,
DANNY

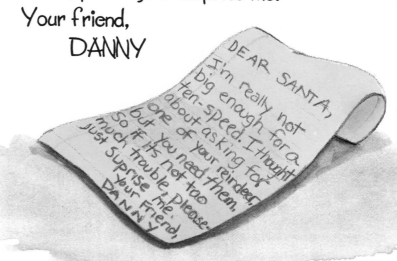

"Now what am I supposed to do, Santa?" Ellie asked.

"Do your best, Little Elf," Santa said. "Think. What would you want for Christmas?"

All Ellie ever wanted was to make toys. Maybe Danny liked to make things too. . .

Ellie wrapped a tool box with a toy hammer and tools, and loaded it in Santa's sleigh. "I hope Danny likes this," she whispered to Rudolph.

While Santa delivered presents, Ellie swept the toy shop and worried. 'If Danny doesn't like his gift, I may never get to be a toy maker.'

Christmas Day, another letter arrived. "It's from Danny!" Santa cried. Ellie held her breath and listened.

Dear Santa,
Thank you so much for the tool box. It was exactly what I wanted!
Love, DANNY

"Yippee!" Ellie and the other elves cheered. "Well,

I'll be a red-nosed reindeer!" exclaimed Santa.

"Looks like we'll have a new toy maker

named Ellie next

Christmas!"